My Mother and the Hungarians

and other small fictions

MY MOTHER
AND THE
HUNGARIANS

and other small fictions

FRANKIE McMILLAN

Canterbury University Press

UNIVERSITY OF
CANTERBURY
Te Whare Wānanga o Waitaha
CHRISTCHURCH NEW ZEALAND

This collection first published in 2016 by

Canterbury University Press
University of Canterbury
Private Bag 4800, Christchurch
New Zealand

universitypress@canterbury.ac.nz
www.cup.canterbury.ac.nz

ISBN 978-1-927145-87-6

A catalogue record for this book is available from the
National Library of New Zealand.

Editor: Emma Neale
Art direction: Aaron Beehre
Design: Aaron Beehre, Gemma Banks

Designed and printed at Ilam Press
Published with the support of Creative New Zealand

ARTS COUNCIL OF NEW ZEALAND TOI AOTEAROA

For Reenie, with love

Acknowledgements

Much of this collection was written during my tenure of the Ursula Bethell Residency in Creative Writing at the University of Canterbury in 2014. I am hugely grateful to the university for awarding me this time and opportunity.

Thanks to Owen Marshall for his generous encouragement, Kerrin Sharpe for forcing me to be better, David Howard for giving me four days of his life and my partner Nicholas Williamson who cheerfully listened to multiple versions of the same story.

Thanks to Catherine Montgomery, publisher at Canterbury University Press, for always being attentive to my many requests. I am enormously thankful for her professionalism. Thanks also to Emma Neale for her editorial advice.

Grateful acknowledgment is made to the editors of *Flash Frontier* where some of these stories appeared in an earlier form.

Contents

The house on Holloway Street

My mother kept boarders like other people kept chooks or stray dogs.
She liked the refugees best with their suitcases, their canvas shoes
tied up with string, their boyish faces and willingness to share a bed
so that if one woke in the night crying, *no shoot, no shoot*, the other
could turn and blanket their sorrows with their old European ways.
My mother said our house was a little window into the twentieth
century and that the cold war would soon be over. She lit a fire down
the backyard and Stefan threw the clothes he had been wearing from
the long plane flight into the flames. The fire snatched at his shorts,
burnt them into ash that blew soft and blossomy about the yard. His
sadness overwhelmed me, his Hungarian breath on the back of my
neck, his foreign arms covered in fine, dark hair. But I liked him well
enough when he took me riding on the bar of his bike. At night we
biked through the streets, the bike lamp whirring against the wheel,
light bouncing over the gravel road and Stefan singing all the way. I
don't remember where we were heading but it was away from the busy
house and hungry men and mixed up washing and quarrels over whose
turn it was to have a bath.

'Your mother wants everything,' Stefan once said, 'she wants the
whole world.'

You are here

It was Morgan's birthday party, Morgan of the blonde plaits and swimming pool right in front of her house and whose skin smelled of corn and her daddy said, 'Right we'll play pin the tail on the donkey,' and you had to look real hard at the donkey pinned to the wall and where his tail was, 'Look hard, girls,' but all I could see was the donkey's eyes that looked mean as though it would go haw haw if the tail got pinned on a chair instead and everyone tried, and Morgan's father had slow and gentle hands so I thought I had nothing to worry about, not really, just step forward with the donkey's tail which was really an old possum tail, and stick it on the body and so I stepped forward with the tea towel tied tight around my eyes and everyone laughing and saying to the right or to the left and more laughing so I just stuck the tail on the first thing I bumped into which was Morgan's daddy and everyone screamed and he said, 'It's ok,' and took the blindfold off and I didn't know where I was because everything had changed, the doors, the windows all the furniture I'd never seen before and I was lost, smack bang in the middle of the birthday party and how would I ever get home again, I didn't know.

The piano learns to swim

It was a rough sea voyage. All the way from Southampton to the Bay of Islands the piano stayed in the hold. From below it heard strange noises: the cry of sea birds, the flap of unfurled sails, the creak and groan of timbers, the squabble of sailors, the trot trot of little children's boots. Sometimes when the piano got lonely, it would play for itself. 'What is that?' cried the children. They turned their ears to the melancholy tinkle.

One day the children visited the piano. Its shadow was enormous and at first they hung back in fright. The piano gently smiled. Such beautiful ivory teeth! Then it played 'Dance of the Sugar Plum Fairy'. The children crept closer, stroking the fine polished wood, marvelling at the shiny brass feet. The next time they saw the piano it was listing on the deck.

A terrible storm. A howling sea. The sky is upside down. The piano is being thrown overboard! The children wave goodbye. The piano lifts its lid … lifts its lid … then plunges into the deep foamy sea. All the way to Aotearoa the piano can be heard. Plonkety plonk as the piano tries first freestyle then breaststroke. Plonkety plonk.

The field guide for lost girls

My grandfather said I fell straight as a plumb bob from the tree. For a while he knelt beside my still body, picking off snapped branches and leaves. The sun climbed higher over the hills. When I finally came around Grandfather said he wasn't sure if it was him or me who was saved. He measured the circumference of my head, traced callipers between my brows, collected my tears. He was pretty sure something had been knocked out of me. Sure enough, it proved to be geography – the maps, the south from north, the east from west, the follow your nose, the straight as the crow flies, the retrace your steps, and the sun always sets.

We never spoke of it. When I got lost crossing the street or made the wrong turn going out the kitchen door, the adults just smiled indulgently. But as I got older I began to find little notes stuffed in my school backpack, in the pocket of my jacket, in the zippered compartment of my bag.

Turn left at the gate until you get to a right hand turn. Follow the seaward route. Mark your distance on the grid. And then there was this one, the one I still carry when walking the streets of strange cities, the one that keeps me from feeling lost. I can just make out Grandfather's writing beside the x.

You are here.

All it takes is a small mistake

When people go on about the view, you say the trees are lovely but
then they want to point out landmarks: 'If you look northwest you'll
see Mt Arthur,' so you pretend you know where northwest is and you
smile or maybe you do a little jiggle on the spot as though there's a
stone in your shoe and that's more pressing than looking northwest
and what you don't want to say is that every morning you wake up
in a house where all the doors and hallways have moved overnight
and the only way forward is to stand in your dressing gown and spin
around until the room rights itself. And then you make a point of
getting the stone out of your shoe and whoever you are with becomes
your best friend, your saviour, you'll slavishly follow them home
because otherwise you could get lost and if they stop for a pee, you
do too so as to not go ahead and ruin the whole trip by climbing the
same hill again. 'We'll head south at this turn,' they say but all you
see are trees. There they are facing you, their trunks still, their arms
frantically waving.

**All it takes is a small mistake, like going
too far from the house in winter**

Folks, the best policy is to never trust any single aid to navigation.
You do not know what you do not know. Some backup method must
be used regularly to check for errors in the primary system. As you
become more and more confident in using a certain navigational
system, it is easy to become dependent on that system. Listen up, folks.
You must understand your system's limitations. Use this understanding
to bring your house – now covered in snow – safely into view.

Asking

'What is a brother-in-law?' I ask my mother. She says it is her sister's husband but I am not so easily fooled. 'What is the tide and what are the waves?' I ask my father. 'It's a matter of perspective,' he says, 'but in the end it's just salty water.'

'And what is landscape?' I press on. My father pours himself a drink. 'Do you need glasses?' he says. 'Is it the trees,' I persist, 'is that all it is?' There is a knock on the door. The Social Welfare have arrived. It's hard to tell whether they are good people or bad people.

'How many people reside in this house?' they ask. 'What are the sleeping arrangements?'

The diaspora of boyfriends

One summer the government failed and a number of men began arriving at our house. They looked like broken-down cowboys with their thin necks and morose faces. They didn't say much but shuffled around on the back doorstep, blowing their noses. 'Where have you come from?' my mother asked but they pointed their hands in vague directions or else gave small sad smiles. Others, like the man in khaki shorts, tried to be helpful. He put a small suitcase on the front step then inquired if there was a man around the place. He could see the roof needed fixing; there was a loose bit of tin that could fly off in a big wind, could even take someone's head off. My mother said she'd never had any trouble with the roof. The man made an odd chewing motion with his mouth. He had small, worn-down teeth, dark bits showing like seeds between the gaps. 'I'm a Jack of all trades,' he finally said.

'Is that so?' my mother said. 'Well, I'm the Queen of Sheba.' The man scratched his head. My mother stared up at the roof.

We'll leave them there, an unchartered distance between them, the wind picking up, the slight rattle of tin under a wide blue sky.

Boarders

… and in this way I developed a tolerance for the odd behaviours of men. They whistled, put up posters of bare-breasted women astride motorbikes and sometimes they cried because they were missing a woman. Then my mother would feed them, barley soup, plates of meat and roly-poly pudding, oozing with burnt jam and topped with cream. *Eat up, eat up,* she cried. Afterwards they staggered to their beds to sleep it off and the house became quiet again.

All this is by way of saying there are ways to manage things. I tell this to my daughters. There they are, striding the tussocky hills, pale legs lit up by the sun. 'What odd men?' they say, 'What are you talking about?' One stops to examine a tiny flowering shrub and I think that one will always save herself. She stands lost in the wonder of the purple star-shaped flower, her head bent low. Then they are both striding up the steep hill again and I struggle to keep up; too soon I will be the Inuit woman left behind in the snow. 'I'm talking,' I yell, 'about how to keep everyone happy.'

When does a hill become a mountain?

Every day I walk the Dry Ridge track but lately the steep hill is
walking me. The land rises to meet my foot, comes up to my knee so
I'm forced to lean forward and take a bigger step. The magpie watches
from a fence post. I pretend it is no big deal, this new thing. I start a
gratitude diary. The light on the silver tussock! My strong legs! The
trees giving and asking for nothing!

**Falling in love the abseiler repeats the same tricky descent,
over and over**

Because he was an abseiler he was used to going back to what he knew
and for that reason his first girlfriend was his only love. He thought
he saw her in a picnic area by Hanging Rock. She sat on a rug, her
red skirt ballooning in the breeze. He let the rope drift through the
descender. As he fell, lichen and rock and inch and toehold, she held
up something from her basket. At first it was just a tiny blur of white
but as he came closer he saw her take a bite of her sandwich. He
wanted to call to her. Of course she would wonder who the man was
on the end of the rope. His bottom looked ridiculous in the harness.
He let himself fall some more.

When there is no one there

Every now and again the woman living in Flat B will ring the police.
She runs out into the street in her nightie then runs inside again.
Sometimes we walk through the house with her. See, we say, there
is no one there. We look under the beds, we check the locks on the
doors. See, we say, no one can get in. But even as we're saying it we
know that someone can always get in, there will always be a way
and she will never be safe just as we are never safe and it may be our
turn to ring the police, to run wild-eyed into the street with all the
neighbours gathering to walk us through the house. See, they will say,
there is no one there.

The woman who wanted to be a homing pigeon

She told her doctor she was tired of being lost. It was a concrete jungle
out there. She had to fight off busy traffic, street hawkers and dogs
just to maintain a straight line. He sat, calmly looking at her. 'But you
got here,' he said. Yes, she had got to his office in Gloucester Street,
but not before going down Worcester Street, up a flight of stairs and
then having to blurt out to startled strangers that she had lost a street.
She said she lacked certain wiring in her brain and that if there were
studies done, on, say, homing pigeons, they might be able to come up
with some way of rewiring her brain, or at the very least, with a pill.

He sat looking at her. She could hear his breathing.

'You're not much help,' she said.

He watched her hesitate by the door. Wondering whether to go left
or right. A few minutes later he peered out from his window to the
pavement below. There she was, walking through a flock of pigeons,
her arms raised; but whether in surrender or in readiness to take off, he
did not know.

Don't move, *apartamento*

Everybody knows a building doesn't have feet. Everybody knows a
street of carefully laid, pale cobblestones doesn't fly apart, the smooth
stones returning to the quarry or the side of the hill from which they
were prised. And everyone knows the moon doesn't swap sides of the
road, it is the road that changes just as it is the river that changes and
not the bridges. But she was not everybody. She was someone who
could at one moment be herself and in the next moment someone
not herself.

They told her she should carry a map. The streets have names, they
said and the names have been there forever. But she had read that
names could change and the Portuguese had their own names, like a
child might have a pet name, a nickname, and the locals kept these
familiar names in their own mouths, secret as dark plums.

My sister and Mr Putin

My sister, Louisa, is in love with President Putin. She watches the
Russian channel on TV which she says is her antidote for the biased
western media but I know she is really hoping for a glimpse of Putin.
Putin riding bare-chested on a horse, Putin playing tennis, Putin
smoking a cigarette on an oligarch's yacht. When I ring to tell her
of my troubles with the neighbours she says, 'What about Putin's
troubles with his!' Then she starts talking about *Ukranian separatists*
and *bilateral agreements.*

My sister has always been smarter than me. She knows things about
Muslims and Jews and Saudi Arabia and who is on whose side. But
I worry about her. She spends time in chat rooms discussing Putin's
policies. She has a framed photo of his impassive face beside her
laptop. I tell her the messages could be recorded by the CIA, her
phone tapped, that she has to stop.

It's coming up to Mr Putin's birthday. I know she'll bake him a cake
and decorate it with 62 candles. I can see her now, the candlelight
flickering over her face, her nostrils lit up in a terrible glory.

The things we lose

When she lost her keys or her cellphone, her bag or even her shoes
and she was in a hurry to go somewhere she'd yell at him to help
her. He'd look in the same bag she'd searched just a minute ago and
find her car keys. Or he'd go to the pile of books on the table and
straightaway find her cellphone. It made her light-headed. She'd kiss
him madly. 'How do you do it?' she'd exclaim. Only very rarely was
he reluctant to look for her lost things and when she sensed that she'd
offer him a reward. 'Find my cellphone,' she'd wink, 'and I'll let loose
all the horses …'

She told him she was losing her marbles. Other people weren't always
losing things. He said not to worry, he didn't mind looking; it was
something he was good at.

She said she would tidy the house, it was the house swallowing up
all the things and for a week she tidied benches, tables, drawers and
bookshelves. Then one day she looked around and he was gone.

She lay alone in her upstairs bedroom staring up at the ceiling. There
was a missing person in her house but how to call him, how to whistle
him back she had no idea. Suddenly she sat up. Shouted out into the
dark. 'There'll be a reward,' she cried.

'There is a sense in which we are all each other's consequences'

She walks through the old city of Lagos. The narrow streets are
crowded with stalls selling cork souvenirs and colourful cloth fish
strung from poles. A man with a blonde child comes hurrying towards
her. The child looks familiar but in the way of dreams she can't be sure.
Mary? Magda? Madeline? The child opens her mouth, forms a single
strange word. It could be 'hullo' or it could be 'help'.

She realises the dream has been cleverly put together to remind her
of all the things she is afraid of. Yet here she is, cobblestones under
her feet, the sharp tang of barbecued fish in the air, the fado singers
singing of lost love from an upstairs balcony. And that holy visitation
of a child that appears whenever she passes the marketplace …?
'Go home,' she wants to tell her.

History is an alternating series of frying pans and fires

– Peter Esterhazy

Do not abandon your clothing in Budapest

The first rule is to look back before the day swallows the shape of things,

that way you will not lose your bearings and as you stagger through

cobbled streets, blinking in the harsh sunlight, follow the late afternoon

crowd, they are heading for the station, they are heading for the ferry

fully clothed. Now look – here is St Stephen's Basilica where the main

altar always faces sunrise and here is where young boys dress as angels

and they cease to be lost, not by returning, but by turning into something else.

Hand me down

My father once told me Stalin was made of melted down other people:
army officers, writers and generals and my mother said he had to
be made out of something and besides he'd never be melted down
for his bronze because they built him with something special inside
so that whatever happened he'd always be in Heroes' Square. *Hello,
Hungarians, I will watch over you forever.* Then they both laughed but
when my grandmother came into the kitchen to poke the fire they
stopped laughing, so later I asked her, is Stalin a good man or a bad
man? and she reared back with the poker. I know he's dead, I said, but
is he a good man or a bad man? and my grandmother dropped the
poker and slapped my face this way and that and I howled and my
father ran in. What did you do to him? he said. And you see, she later
regretted this or maybe my father had words with her because that
evening she took an old blue skirt, ripped it to pieces and said she was
making something new for me. All night I watched the light under
the door, hoping whatever she sewed would do the trick and turn me
into someone else.

Everyone has a Stalin story to tell (or not)
Oct 23rd 1956

I went to the uprising in my pyjamas. My father hauled me out of bed and told me to get into the back seat of his taxi. 'Hurry!' he yelled. Then he was driving fast through District 14, shouting at the radio. I poked my head out the window. It was foggy outside but I could still see Stalin from three blocks away, so I knew we were heading towards Heroes' Square. The next thing we were zig-zagging through a crowd, people shouting and banging the bonnet of the taxi. My father was laughing as we lurched past all the statues towards Stalin. I stared straight ahead. I couldn't make sense of it. People were crawling like ants over the big bronze statue. 'You want to see?' said my father. He swung me up on the roof. 'They're taking him down.'

My father said it was history. He said I was the only boy in the world to be standing on a cab roof and watching Stalin fall. I think he wanted me to be thinking noble thoughts but after a while all I could think of was that it was taking forever and how would they ever get the ladders all the way to his head?

They put big steel ropes around Stalin's neck. My father counted twenty-eight trucks pulling the ropes. A man with a moustache stood at the front waving a flag. Then the ropes tightened, engines roared and the man pulled his jacket over his head to hide from all the smoke and dust. Stalin stood his ground. More men came running with axes and crowbars and they hacked and hammered at his body. Some people began cheering. 'Hang in there little Joseph,' they yelled as

the ropes began to strain and tighten again and all the trucks roaring
their hardest, back ends raised in the air. An old woman in a blue-
chequered headscarf pushed past my father and at first I thought it
was my grandmother come to take me home but then she opened her
mouth. 'Horse dick! Horse dick!' she cried. 'He'll win, he always does!'

Then she saw me standing on the cab roof in my pyjamas and while
she was gaping at me I stood still as a statue so she would never know
whose side I was on.

We were there a long time. 'Don't go to sleep,' my father said as sparks
from the blowtorches flew into the dark.

They cut him off at the boots. Stalin swung around then hit the
ground and bounced. The earth shook and dust rose in the air. For a
while people went very quiet. Then some crowded around to spit on
Stalin's big face and others ran away. My father lifted me down from
the roof. He gripped my shoulders. 'Always, always remember this
day,' he said. His voice was hoarse with all the yelling. 'But never, *never*
speak of it.'

And then he was standing by his taxi and people were singing, all
except the old woman who suddenly darted forward and stole away
with a piece of Stalin's finger.

'Gaiety is the most outstanding feature of the Soviet Union'

We last visited Stalin just before our teacher got married. She said Stalin was her father, she told him everything, all her news and sometimes she asked his advice and we all looked up to the huge towering statue to see if his great mouth moved but his face stayed still, though Louis said if you kept staring at his face long enough it would become whatever you wanted it to be. It was Louis who told me Stalin's boots were standing right on top of where a church altar had been. He made a slit gesture under his neck. 'Don't say I said, otherwise I'll have to kill you.'

'The Happiest Sculptor'
Sándor Mikus

Will it be the beckoning hand or the hand on the heart? Or the Napoleonic gesture – a hand slipped into the jacket? What best suits our infallible leader? Perhaps what Giotto did in his fresco, Christ extending his arm to greet his disciples? The thing about the hand keeps me awake. I lie in bed studying my own hand, bringing it slowly towards my face. My fingers perform a ballet in the air. Then I close my hand over my face. How quickly darkness comes! My wife shifts in the bed. 'Sándor,' she warns. She wants the lamp turned off but I'm not done yet. I try cupping my hand in a gentle beckon. Yes. No. I switch off the light. Try focusing on something else. Stalin's military tunic. I'll have it buttoned, as usual, to the chin. I'm almost asleep when something occurs to me. 'What is it now?' my wife says. 'The shadow!' I yell. 'Jesus. Think of the shadow of his outstretched arm.'

The marketplace
Oct 23rd 1956

When he sees the taxi it's as though God is on his side. A friend helps
him haul the giant hand through the crowd and into the back seat.
He remembers a kid scrambling into the front but the kid doesn't say
anything. The taxi driver throws his cigarette butt out the window.
Slams the car into reverse. The suspension groans as he takes off,
swerving to avoid the debris littered over the ground. The man in the
back stares at the broken hand. Stalin's broken hand, the metal fingers
twisted and torn but still Stalin's hand. The driver looks in the rear
vision mirror. He speaks in Hungarian, slowly as if the language is still
new to him. 'What will you do with it?' he says. The man laughs. He
leans over into the front. The words aren't yet in his mouth, he will
have to wait twenty-five years for that. Instead he will gently reach
out, ruffle the kid's hair.

He will live high off the hog in Vienna

Such a huge hole he digs that night, the fog coming in, gunfire in
the streets, his wife calling to him, she wants to leave, she's packed a
suitcase but he still has the great hand to cover, the dirt slides off the
edges and no matter how hard he works, throwing spadefuls on top,
sweat pouring down his arms, the handle slippery, those giant fingers
wait, ready to pluck at his trouser leg, and to the sound of Bartók's
symphony, he will, if he's not careful, be part of the dénouement.

The worm as witness

It spoke in a broken voice, the metal whined at night, the nails never grew, it was a long way from home, it missed the other hand.

Yes, this was the left hand.

Yes, we heard the attack … men with sledgehammers, crow bars, hammers and such. The fingers scraped the cobbles as it was dragged away. We had to cover our ears.

Yes, we heard the earth break open.

We were cold. We kept hugging each other. The spades came down and then there was blinding light. None of us knew what to do.

We thought someone would come back for the hand. When we heard the Russian tanks come back we said now we must brace ourselves. Now they will carry the hand away. But no one came.

Who put the hand there? We can explain that, but then you would understand our explanation, not what we said.

Why did we not report it? Because things always change. That is the earth's way. Have you not heard the saying? *In time, even grass becomes milk.*

Small occupations

My mother's friend rings in the morning. 'What are your Hungarians up to?' she says and my mother replies her Hungarians are out looking for work. The friend says hers have been restless, they kept her awake last night with their drinking and fighting. 'Go on,' says my mother. Her friend says she thinks one is a Communist, he snuck in with the others but they have found him out. 'Go back to Mother Russia,' she heard the men yell, 'she will protect you, ha, ha.' My mother says she has good Hungarians, they are just boys really, in their white shorts and sneakers. 'They love America,' she says.

My mother's friend has been given bikes for the Hungarians. 'Have the Red Cross given you bikes?' she says and my mother says yes, they love their bikes, in the weekend they ride to New Brighton to look at the sea. They like to feel sand through their fingers, she explains. Then her friend says something has been puzzling her but she doesn't like to ask. Where are all the Hungarian girls, all the women …? Were they shot? My mother laughs, haven't you heard, she says, they went to Wellington, they're used to the big cities and her friend says that is a pity because if they were here they would calm her boys down. And then my mother says she has to get off the phone but they will talk again soon and they do talk again over and over but my mother says only good things about the Hungarians and her only complaint is that they have taken up chewing gum and leave wads of it under the kitchen table.

Night talk

At Holloway Street some of us sleep in single beds, three to a room
with a fireplace, a piano and a picture of Mt Egmont on the wall;
some sleep together, while others sleep in baches down the backyard
where chooks scratch in the dirt and when quince trees drop heavy
fruit on the tin roof Stefan shouts, 'They're coming!' and Imre sits in
his underwear on the side of the bed and says he will kill Stefan if he
wakes him up one more time, he will fill his throat with plums and
some of us say maybe Wellington would have been better, think about
it – cafés, coffee and cake and playing violins and joining societies of
this and that but others say you are dreaming, everything you want is
right here, so many jobs and all you have to do is forget whatever is
gone and pretty soon we will speak good English and all the beautiful
New Zealand girls running, running to meet us.

First the Russians, then the Jews

Some of us remember the start of it all, our ears pressed to Radio Free
Europe, then running along the Pest with makeshift placards and
the cry of the crowd when the soldiers threw off their military shirts
to march with us and others remember the late night celebrations,
fucking with a stranger in an upstairs room, lights and gunfire strafing
the night and saying that nobody, of all the millions of people in the
world, was doing any better than what we were doing right now and
others remember Hajdúnánás when the cry went up to get the Jews,
stone their shop windows and a few of us tried to stop the crowd
from hanging a boy at the back of the gymnasium, tried to pull the
chains from their hands but the crowd was chanting *Aushwitz is too
good for you* and the boy stood still, terror in his eyes, and though some
of us said they knew nothing of this and the uprising was our finest
hour, still the nightmares came and a truck on the street, a milk truck
could rattle us from sleep and we woke upright in the dark and had
to tell ourselves, now we are refugees, now we live in the West, in
Holloway Street and some of us were calmed but others felt remorse
and wondered what overtook them that day at the gymnasium, when
they who had suffered so much now joined the crowd to see another
suffer so.

The West opens its arms

We got a good welcome, we all agree about that and we nodded as if
we understood everything and went to our rooms pretending not to
be surprised the doors opened the wrong way and we sat on the beds
and wondered if the food would be the same as the reception camp;
whether we'd ever see *kávé* and *kuglóf* and *vadas hús* and *lescó* again and
Stefan said count your blessings, his grandfather died through the lack
of a potato and others said true, their grandmother lost two children
through lack of a single piece of bread and Louis said stop talking like
peasants, a man needs to fill more than his belly and where were the
concerts, the intellectual life and the goddamn street lights and the
others ran about closing the windows as though a snowstorm were
coming and when the woman of the house, whose name nobody could
pronounce, opened the door to see us sitting on our beds she laughed
and said come outside and get some fresh air, and we raised our heads
and dumbly nodded and in another month we would raise our heads
and say, we're ok, right as rain, box of birds we are.

. . . .

Mostly my mother cooks vegetables in a pressure cooker, a little
triangular apartment for each vegetable. The big pot blows steam
into the kitchen and rattles and shakes on the stove. Today it blows
its top with a terrible screaming noise and vegetables shoot all over
the ceiling. József runs outside, a cigarette trembling in his lips. Stefan
runs up and down the hallway. 'Taxi!' he shouts, the only word he

knows. Even when my mother comes running home from the neighbours and stands in the kitchen doorway laughing at the potatoes, the carrots, the gleaming cabbage hanging from the ceiling, the Hungarians are suspicious. Such a terrible waste of food and why is my mother laughing like that, doubled over, clutching her skirt.

Stopover

Not all of us wanted New Zealand girls, Louis and Imre said they
wanted girls from their homeland because who else would know
where they had come from, who else could speak their language, sob
with them while listening to Bartók or remembering October 23
and who else could they walk arm in arm with or kiss without them
pulling away, *oh, not in public, please?* Others said yes, but who else is as
burdened by the past as one of us, has night terrors, missing parents, a
stone forever in their shoe and back and forth the argument went and
always after a while would come the story of the stopover in Calcutta;
how two of the boys thought the prostitutes were a free social service
like the white shirts and shoes, the sports goods from the Red Cross,
and all of us laughed and slapped our thighs remembering the run
half-naked to the plane, all except József who stood at the bench
peeling potatoes, their white cheerful bodies piling up in the sink.

Mostly

'How are your Hungarians fitting in?' my mother says. She's on the
phone to her friend again using the same careful voice she uses with
foreigners. My mother says hers are fitting in so well that people
are often surprised when they open their mouths. 'Oh you're not
from here,' mimics my mother 'where do you come from?' *Budapest?*
Budapest? She looks up from the phone and I duck my head. 'They
don't even know where it is,' she says. Then she tells her friend the city
is divided in two, Buda and Pest … isn't that something! A long pause
and I just about give up on the conversation when I hear her mention
József's name. 'The neighbour thought he was a dentist,' she says.
'Yes,' my mother says, 'she said *dentist*. I don't know,' my mother sighs,
'perhaps she thought refugees would be barefoot and ragged …' My
mother stands, looks at herself in the hall mirror. She doesn't know I'm
watching her. She opens her mouth to inspect her pretty teeth.

The one who is saved

Who is your favourite Hungarian I ask my mother but she laughs,
that question is too difficult she says, so then I say, *try*, and I pull her
skirt, *try*, because then I will know something about her even if she
doesn't know it herself, but she doesn't have a favourite, just like she
doesn't have a favourite child, but I say imagine if all the Hungarians
were drowning, all waving their arms above their heads and wild waves
crashing over them, who would you save? And my mother pauses from
twiddling the dials on the radio and says what's brought this on? And
I say they would all be yelling for help so who would you save and
my mother says, just one? and I say yes, just one and I see my mother
swimming towards József, dark floppy hair streaked over his white
face and his mouth desperate and salty, but just before she gets to
him Stefan waves her over, help, help, and I look at my mother as she
bends her head closer to the radio, she can hear Selwyn Toogood, her
favourite quiz show and By Hokey, he exclaims, his big voice flooding
the kitchen, What should she do, New Zealand?

It's arm wrestle time again

Imre and Sándor lie on their stomachs facing each other, elbows
propped straight. Imre spits on his palms and Sándor spits on his
palms and their fingers interlock, they gently rock arms, but just before
they start József walks around them, steps over their bare, hairy legs
to get the china cabinet out of their way and then it's *321 GO* and
Sándor hurls his arm against Imre's arm and Imre holds steady, his
Adam's apple bulges, his toes dig into the carpet and they all shout
'*Igen! Igen!*' and József gets on his knees to see if an elbow has moved
and then a roar goes up as Imre suddenly pushes Sándor's arm over
flat to the ground and no one saw it coming and they all whoop and
laugh and József tries to straighten the carpet because now my mother
is standing at the door. She is saying something about lunch wrappers,
did they bring them home for her to use again and she keeps standing
there, demanding attention, letting everyone know she is the true boss
of Holloway Street.

**On Sundays the Hungarians do not sit in their cars
and stare at the sea**

They ride their Red Cross bikes to visit their friends.

They carry presents of cheese on their carriers.

Everyone talks at the same time.

They laugh and sob. 'Always remember!' they shout.

They laugh and sob. 'Forget the past!' they shout.

They ride home, their pale faces peering through the dark.

'… nobody's here, only a blackbird burns
its feathers in the distance …'

What I wanted to understand was their Hungarianness. I watched
their surprised faces as they tasted salted butter for the first time,
watched them looking past their dinner plates and over to the stove
as if there might be something different coming, watched them leave
the bathroom, hair dripping wet, the fine hairs on their arms sleek as
a seal's, their bare feet leaving damp imprints on the hallway carpet
and always a faint smell of what I imagined was gunpowder in their
room mixed with the lonely smell of suitcase. And though I knew I
shouldn't, I flew into their rooms as soon as they went out riding on
their bikes and I stood there peering at their socks, their underpants
hurled on the floor, and sometimes under the bed gathering dust and
I sniffed their dirty clothes then opened their top drawers to look
at letters I could never fold straight again and when they returned
on their bikes, wheels crunching the gravel driveway, I was already
perched up in the quince tree, singing loudly, 'God Save the Queen',
the only song I knew by heart.

In New Zealand there are many parties to belong to

Every now and again my mother says she is going to throw a party. *Throw a party.* My father must never know so if I should happen to see him on the street there is to be no mention of it. She draws up lists of food and people to invite and then she walks through the house as if seeing it for the first time, staring at a picture on the wall or rearranging the blue velvet chairs in the front room. It'll be good for the boys she says and they can bring other Hungarians but not Mrs Riley's ones who drink and sob noisily in the kitchen and she'll clear the front room for dancing, get the piano tuned and if the Hungarians want to do arm wrestling they can do it outside and maybe her uncle could get her a crayfish and she'd get her sister to make a Madeira cake, no hang on, a pavlova. But what happens is that a few days later she goes off the idea and has to ring her sister: 'I'm postponing the party.' This becomes so familiar that when she begins again to talk excitedly about a party I soon forget about it until one day I get home from school and see my mother, slightly tipsy, swinging from the rotary clothesline while strangers cheer her on. She wears a cotton frock with red roses around the hem and kicks her bare legs in a way that makes the world feel strange.

The Hungarians are by themselves in the front room, talking about the government. They wear their best white shirts. József stands at the window watching my mother pedal her legs through the air. He turns towards me. There is something he doesn't understand. He gestures with his palms.

'It's a party,' I say. I pronounce it slow and clear. P a r t y.

The Hungarians roll up their shirt sleeves

They like to show off their arm muscles. 'Feel,' they invite us.

My big sister steps forward. Sándor tenses his arm and she reaches up to touch the smooth, hard bulge. She nods solemnly then moves on to Edvard, József and Imre. They try to look fierce, to pump themselves up, to be the strongest. Imre springs up and down on his white sandshoes, throwing punches in the air. When my sister gets to him he tenses his arm so hard the veins in his neck bulge. She steps back to consider the line up. When she points to Edvard he laughs, throwing back his head to show the gold fillings in his teeth. Now it is my turn to see who has the biggest arm muscle, who is the strongest one, but just before I do my sister points to their muscles.

M u s s o l l i n i she pronounces. I don't know where she gets this word from – it sounds like something from the sea, but I keep a straight face.

M u s s o l l i n i they repeat.

The Hungarians swallow every bit of language we give them.

Borders

The kids at school ask if our Hungarians are hungry but I don't say, instead I draw the shape of a mouth with a wobbly upper lip, *this is a map of Hungary* and when they ask for a swear word I tell them what I hear Stefan yell in the night, *kuss kuss,* and the kids think it means kissing and they walk around the playground ready to bail someone up by the water fountain, *kuss kuss* they cry but after a while they get bored and want more stories. So I tell them how Imre, Stefan and Istvan take my sisters and me for rides on their bikes at night. I don't say we just go wherever the bike lamp leads us nor that in the dark their Hungarian breath rises like steam and we cling to the cold handlebars as the bike shudders downhill over the railway bridge to Sydenham. Nor do I tell them how our father waits outside his house and drops coins into their hands as we ride past and when I look back through the dark he is still there waving to us as if we were another country.

No sooner

… does my mother arrive home from her afternoon shift at the glove
factory, prop her bike in the shed, pull off her head scarf, stand in the
kitchen making a small whistling noise between her teeth, than József
is beside her pointing out the peeled potatoes, the cleared table, the
pile of dictionaries and paper from the night before stacked neatly on
top of the fridge.

'New Zealand women will be very happy with you,' she says.

No sooner does my mother see that József has done her washing,
including the blood-stained underpants she shoved to the back of her
wardrobe, than she leaps from her bike to pull them from the line.

'New Zealand women …' she begins. Her face is flushed. She wants
to say more but it's tricky, untying her scarf with one hand, folding her
stained washing over and over with the other.

Never him

On the twelfth night my big sister wakes me up. There is a knocking
sound on the wall outside; it could be our father, he could be about to
throw bags of Mackintosh's toffees on our beds before disappearing
into the dark again. So for a while we just lie there and then my sister
says it's not him and I should look out the window, she'll hold my legs
tight so nobody can haul me away. So I do and through the dark I can
see the neighbour's Christmas tree all lit up in their living room and
my sister is pulling on my nightie, 'What can you see?' and I'm just
about to tell her when there's another thump against the wall and a
pair of legs drop down from my mother's window and I pull my head
in quick before the man can see me and the next thing the front door
opens and someone walks quietly down the hall to murder us and we
dive under the blankets and the trick when you're frightened is to close
your eyes, to go straight to sleep until the morning, but then my sister
whispers something, her breath hot and anxious in my ear. 'What do
you want for Christmas?' she says.

The happy word

I can see the kitchen light under the doorway and hear the murmured voices. My mother is teaching the Hungarians again. 'One ticket please to the Square. How are you today? I am well, thank you. I am ok, thank you. I'm right as rain, thank you.' Sometimes the Hungarians draw pictures: stick-like figures with heads too big for their bodies, and they sit in buses waving out to everyone. I want to get out of bed and join everyone in the kitchen with its night smell of coffee and the continent and big dictionaries but I know my mother will put me back to bed again so I lie there but I can't sleep. The wind is knocking the branches of a tree against the roof so I tiptoe to the door and my mother is explaining about uniforms, the bus driver wears a uniform but he doesn't have a gun or anything and Stefan says he sees uniforms everywhere and then József says we are at the bottom of the world and my mother says a bad man is not going to come all the way over from Eastern Europe to get you, that is a lot of travel. And then she tells Stefan if he is afraid of walking through the Square at night or taking a bus, he can call a taxi. Stefan nods. His arm shoots out like a salute. 'Taxi!' he cries. It is his happy word.

The Iron Fist, the Iron Curtain, etc.

Mr Holyoake comes on the radio sounding as if he is wearing white
gloves. He says the West has opened its arms to Hungary and 1,000
refugees have come to New Zealand, then he says something about
the Iron Curtain and how they have made a tear in it and I think of
the big red curtain at the Tivoli, how it cranks in little jerks across
the screen at interval and I think of my mother and the Hungarians
sitting there watching the ad – 'Time to light up a Capstan', only my
mother doesn't smoke, she has a box of Queen Anne chocolates on
her knee and they laugh when they see the long queue for ice creams;
the boy with a tray of cones who can never keep up and then the big
red curtain moves and the Hungarians stare straight ahead as it slowly
gathers its folds to jerk back into place.

'… and in a flash it seemed all the unliving we had loved were flying overhead …'

We did not have much; most of what we carried was in our heads, a smell, a snatch of song, our mother's face, but we had our suitcases and Imre had letters and we had each other of course, though some would say let's not gnaw that bone again. And though some of us shared a room or a bed it was *our* little space in the world and a place where Stefan hid when the Hungarian Welfare officer came with his briefcase, his smell of government and questions. A place where Sándor stared at girlie magazines, hand flapping under the blankets, and where Louis turned his face to the wall and hummed all he could remember of *Madárka, madárka* while József cut his toenails and stuffed newspaper into the tip of his good shoes every night.

When we noticed someone had been in our room we were angry: we noted what had changed, a drawer had been opened, a bed had been sat on, a suitcase moved. Imre said it was a child and Sándor said yes, but who has told the child to do this and József said, children here are different and Imre said, you can take poison to that! His father would beat him for less, then hang him by his collar from a tree branch and a minute later a terrible look came over his face and he slumped on the bed and we felt what he felt, that our fathers were missing, there was no one to give us advice, to shout this is the way, no one to say when we stumbled and wept, 'Ah, bogárkám, why are you giving drinks to the mice?'

My mother is becoming a Hungarian

She won't answer the phone in case it's Social Welfare and if we see
a van coming slowly down the street and stopping briefly outside
the house we are to tell her straight away. It could be the radio man
checking on our signal. He has special equipment to pick up on who
has a radio in the street and whether they have paid the licence. My
mother says she never listens to the radio anyway. She smiles at the
man with a clipboard in his hand. 'Even if I had a radio,' she adds,
'I wouldn't listen to it.'

Before the Social Welfare comes, she covers the fridge with an old
woollen blanket and piles folded washing on top. She hangs a big coat
over the phone in the hallway. They ask her terrible questions but she
has all the answers ready. No, she does not have a boyfriend, no she
does not sleep with a man. No, her husband does not pay maintenance
for the children, never has. And if they ask her about the boarders
she will tell the truth. She is helping the refugees. Yes, they pay her
board each week. But the size of her grocery bill! There is no money in
Hungarians, she will say.

The world has become bigger than my head can ever hold

Sometimes I wonder about the world before I was born and how it
worked without me; how my mother and father could walk down
Colombo Street, laughing and not even knowing about me, or
worrying where I was and then I have scary thoughts about beginnings
and endings and that I might die and it's worse at night when my
mother is busy cooking the dinner or behind the closed kitchen door
with the lessons. One thing I know is I don't have those scary thoughts
when we go biking with the Hungarians and I'm not afraid of the
cold, dark streets, my feet getting caught in the chain, a dog with devil
eyes running across the road, and I'm not afraid of the train hurtling
across Moorhouse Ave, billowing smoke even though the Hungarians
get off their bikes and settle themselves with a cigarette, nor am I
afraid if they visit their friends who crowd around the bikes laughing
and sometimes pinching my cheek and even on the short cut home by
the river with its deep smell of water rats and the Hungarians shouting
at them I'm never afraid, but when I wake in the night and the light is
still on under the kitchen door and I peer through the keyhole and see
József and my mother dancing then I start to worry about beginnings
and endings all over again.

'… and suddenly across the wall a shadow fell …'

I don't even hear the bikes come back. Now the back door opens and the Hungarians are already in the hallway. I hide under the nearest bed and I can see their bare legs and sandshoes and József's shoes, the brogue ones with a hundred holes in the leather and next thing someone sits heavily on the bed and the wire frame snags my hair and I'm pulling my hair loose and dust is in my throat and the Hungarians are talking their language, not English but I hear my mother's name and they laugh and József swears and leaves the room and the legs in front of me pause then shift back and forth over the floor, back and forth and then suddenly the legs stop and there is silence.

A face appears under the bed. Imre stares at me. He reaches out, pulls my foot and I slide out in a trail of dust. The Hungarians gather around me. 'A spy! Spy!' they shout as I rush red-faced from the room.

Soon the war will be over

My mother will return to the kitchen.

The Hungarians will stop yelling.

They will say, come for a ride on the bike.

They will say, who is the fastest Hungarian?

I will say it is József, Stefan, Imre, Sándor.

I will say it is Gergo, Edvard, Istvan and Louis.

All their names as we hurtle down the bridge.

The geography of a name

Some of us said what use is a long foreign name in New Zealand;
better to be like our ancestors who stole the town's name for
themselves as they fled but others said their name meant something to
them. Yes said Istav, he was named after his uncle burnt in the ovens
so that made him a dead man walking, ha ha, but Louis said that is
not so funny. Here is funny. How do two Hungarian Jews introduce
themselves to each other? 'My name was Feldman. What was yours?'

And then Sándor threw down his girlie magazine and said he
wouldn't be naming himself after some little town. 'Hullo I am Sándor
Eketahuna, hullo I am Sándor Takaka.' He was named after the great
Petöfi Sándor! His mother had been reading *The Wine Drinker* as she
lay on the bed when a bird smashed into the window and slid down
the pane leaving a smatter in the snow in a perfect S shape. The others
said, 'Yes, yes, we have heard that before,' but they all agreed – their
first names came from writers, film makers, composers. From saints,
from kings, the holy ones. And then there was silence until József said,
'Well, depends on whether you want to fit in or not,' and Louis swore
in perfect Kiwi: 'Bugger to that. Am I a brick or stone to be fitted in?'

So it happened like this. In our new country, we became the one name,
'the Hungarians'. It filled up the mouths of the New Zealanders and it
was like a tuning fork, we could gauge people's response to the name –
whether their faces showed curiosity and warmth or clouded with fear
and when their fearful questions came, 'What are you, Hungarians,

are you Communist, are you Jew, what do you call yourselves?' some of us put up our fists and others pretended not to understand or copied the Kiwi way and we laughed, we praised the weather, the sport, the churches, the mutton and we held our Magyar tongues. But in our dreams we sometimes heard our mothers calling us. Our names! Across oceans, continents, borders, the sound insistent as a wingbeat, and we woke in the dark, crying, 'I am here. I am here!'

After the Hungarians, my mother takes up gardening

She turns a blind eye to the naked man at the bottom of the garden.
He is an elderly Dutchman and loves sunning himself, his body turned
to the sky.

We watch the weather. When clouds roll in, the first faint spots of
rain, the Dutchman will rise from his wooden bench and disappear
inside his sleep-out. 'Call him,' we beg our mother. He is a mystery,
a bronze being, his skin so burnished we think of polished saddles,
the whiff of warm bicycle tyres. 'What do you eat?' we want to ask.
'Where do you come from?'

The Dutchman brews coffee on a little Primus stove. The coffee
grounds smell rich and cause our hearts to beat a little faster. The silver
pot flashes in the sun. His clogs shuffle through the long grass to the
tap hanging from a post. There is a word he says, over and over again.

No one else has a naked man living at the bottom of their garden. No
one else has a mother who turns a blind eye. And no one else grows
giant sunflowers, their faces heavy with happiness.

But if in surrender or about to take off

My sister rings to tell me she's just seen Imre. All this time he'd been living just a few streets away from her. He was married to a friend of a friend's cousin. She was lucky to catch him at the airport; he was on his way to live with his son in Brisbane. 'What did he say,' I ask, 'about us?'

My sister reports back that our mother was 'very kind'. We both laugh. It's a relief to hear this. 'What about József?' I ask. József who could almost have been our father …? My sister says he went back to Budapest after the fall of Communism but couldn't settle, everything had changed, even the street names. Then he came back and lived in Wellington. He was an architect, she said, not a dentist. I don't know where the dentist thing came in. We both agree it was probably József who scaled my mother's wall at night. 'Did Imre know?' I ask, 'Did the others know?' but my sister says they had bigger things to worry about.

It was hard for them, fitting in, she said. Every day trying to figure things out … Then she starts up a political analysis of why the West encouraged the 1956 uprising but didn't help at the crucial hour. 'What else did Imre say about our mother?' I ask. For some reason I need to know how she was kind to the refugees, was it her patient teaching of English, was it her sympathetic manner when Stefan and Imre fled to their rooms if anyone in a uniform appeared? My sister hasn't finished with the Suez Canal crisis and it's while she's giving a general overview of the situation that I realise something.

'Do you ever get lost?' I butt in. 'You know, in a city …' I already know she doesn't. She flies alone to strange countries, is perfectly at ease navigating bridges and bypasses and borders. She has a wide-angle view of things, whereas I have a close up view of footpaths, of fissures, of feet, one foot following the other, not knowing where but having to believe the not-knowing might just be the only flight of reason.

Notes

'The piano learns to swim': This piece appears in my first poetry collection, *Dressing for the Cannibals;* because of its pertinent theme, it resurfaces here.

'The field guide for lost girls': This name carries echoes of the title *The Field Guide to Getting Lost* by Rebecca Solnit.

'All it takes is a small mistake, like going too far from the house in winter': Found text. Source: *The American Practical Navigator: an epitome of navigation* by Nathaniel Bowditch.

'When there is no one there': Influenced by Lydia Davis's *Collected Stories.*

'My sister and Mr Putin': 'Her nostrils lit up in a terrible glory' – this line is a variation from Job 39:20, the King James Bible.

'There is a sense in which we are all each other's consequences': The title comes from Wallace Stegner, *All the Little Live Things.*

'Do not abandon your clothing in Budapest': The last line borrows a quotation from Cabeza de Vaca, a Spanish explorer of the New World, 1490–1560.

'Gaiety is the most outstanding feature of the Soviet Union': The title is a quotation from Josef Stalin.

'The Happiest Sculptor': The press dubbed Sándor Mikus 'The Happiest Hungarian Sculptor' following his winning proposal for the Stalin statue in Budapest. Altogether the monument reached 59 feet.

'The marketplace': The line 'He will live high off the hog in Vienna' was said by the Hungarian writer who sold Stalin's bronze nose to an American millionaire. The sale enabled him to live comfortably off the proceeds. Source: *Imagining Postcommunism: Visual Narratives of Hungary's 1956 Revolution*, by Beverly A. James.

'The worm as witness': The abbreviated line 'In time, even grass becomes milk' comes from Charan Singh, former Prime Minister of the Republic of India.

'First the Russians, then the Jews': Source: *Tainted Revolution*, short video by Arnold van Bruggen/Prospektor (http://www.prospektor.nl/film/tainted-revolution/?lang=en)

'... nobody's here, only a blackbird burns its feathers in the distance ...': The title is borrowed from a line by Hungarian poet, Attila József.

'... and in a flash it seemed all the unliving we had loved were flying overhead ...': The title comes from 'Peace, Dread' a poem by Miklós Radnóti (1909–1944).

'... and suddenly across the wall a shadow fell ...': The title comes from 'Peace, Dread' a poem by Miklós Radnóti (1909–1944).

'But if in surrender or about to take off': The last line is influenced by a quotation from Tolstoy in *War and Peace*.

Helpful background reading for this collection included Ann Beaglehole's 'Facing the Past: Looking back at refugee childhood in New Zealand' (doctoral thesis, Victoria University of Wellington, 1990) and *Imagining Postcommunism: Visual Narratives of Hungary's 1956 Revolution* by Beverly A. James (Houston: Texas A&M University Press, 2005).